D0272787

For Holly and Tess –
the giggliest twins in the world

Big Foot copyright © Frances Lincoln Limited 2002
Text and illustrations copyright © M.P. Robertson 2002

First published in Great Britain in 2002 by
Frances Lincoln Limited, 4 Torriano Mews
Torriano Avenue, London NW5 2RZ

www.franceslincoln.com

All rights reserved

No part of this publication may be reproduced, stored in a retrieval
system, or transmitted, in any form, or by any means, electrical,
mechanical, photocopying, recording or otherwise without
the prior written permission of the publisher or a licence
permitting restricted copying. In the United Kingdom
such licences are issued by the Copyright Licensing Agency,
90 Tottenham Court Road, London W1P 9HE.

British Library Cataloguing in Publication Data
available on request

ISBN 0-7112-1945-1

Set in Clearface

Printed in Singapore
9 8 7 6 5 4 3 2 1

# BiG Foot

## M.P. Robertson

FRANCES LINCOLN

There's a creature lurking in the deep dark woods.
At night he sings his sad song to an ice cold moon.

One fat moon night I heard his song.
I opened my window and played a tune
to the trees. There came a sad reply.
He was very lonely. He needed a friend!

I climbed out into the crisp cold. He had left a trail
of footprints. He had very big feet – even bigger
than my dad's. I will call him 'Big Foot', I decided.

I followed his trail as it wove deeper
and deeper into the dark woods.

Snow began to fall silently. It laid a white blanket
over the trail. I would never find Big Foot now.

I turned towards home, but each tree looked
the same as the last.

The forest had swallowed me up.

I sat down and shivered beneath the ice cold moon.

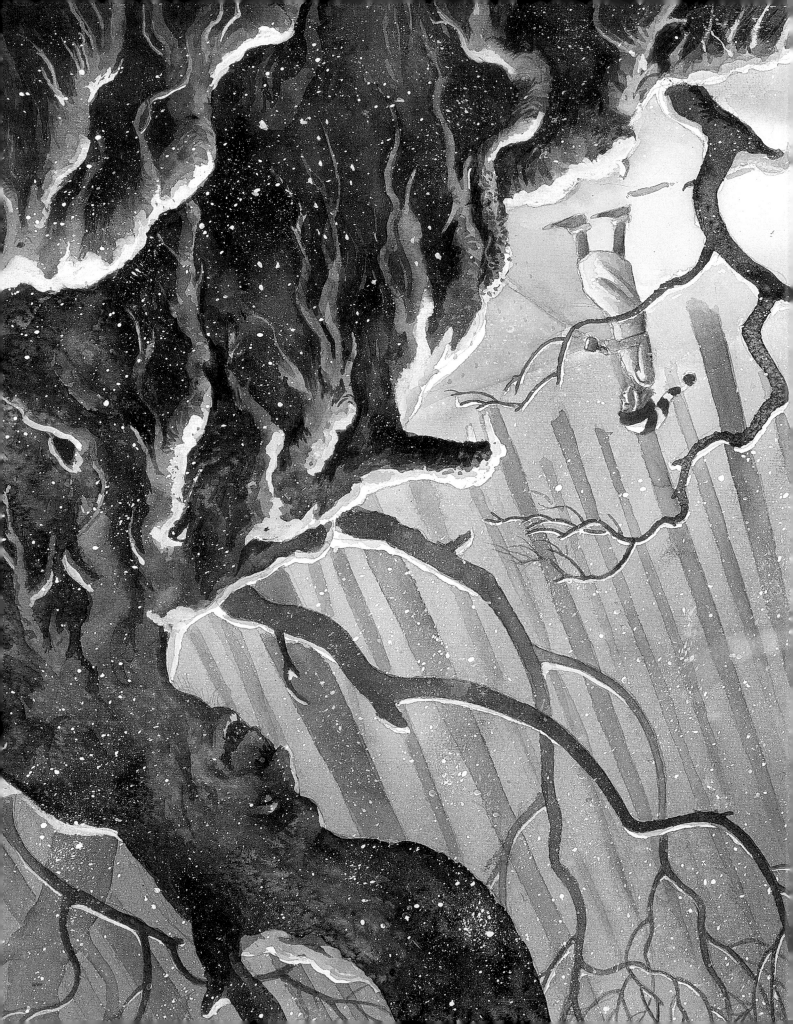

I took out my flute and played a warming tune.

   Then suddenly something stirred. Something BIG…
something HAIRY! As tall as a tree but with gentleness
in his eyes.

   It was Big Foot.

   "I'm lost," I sobbed. "Can you show me the way home?"
   He brushed an icicle tear from my cheek, then lifted
me on to his broad shoulders, and together we bounded
through the trees.

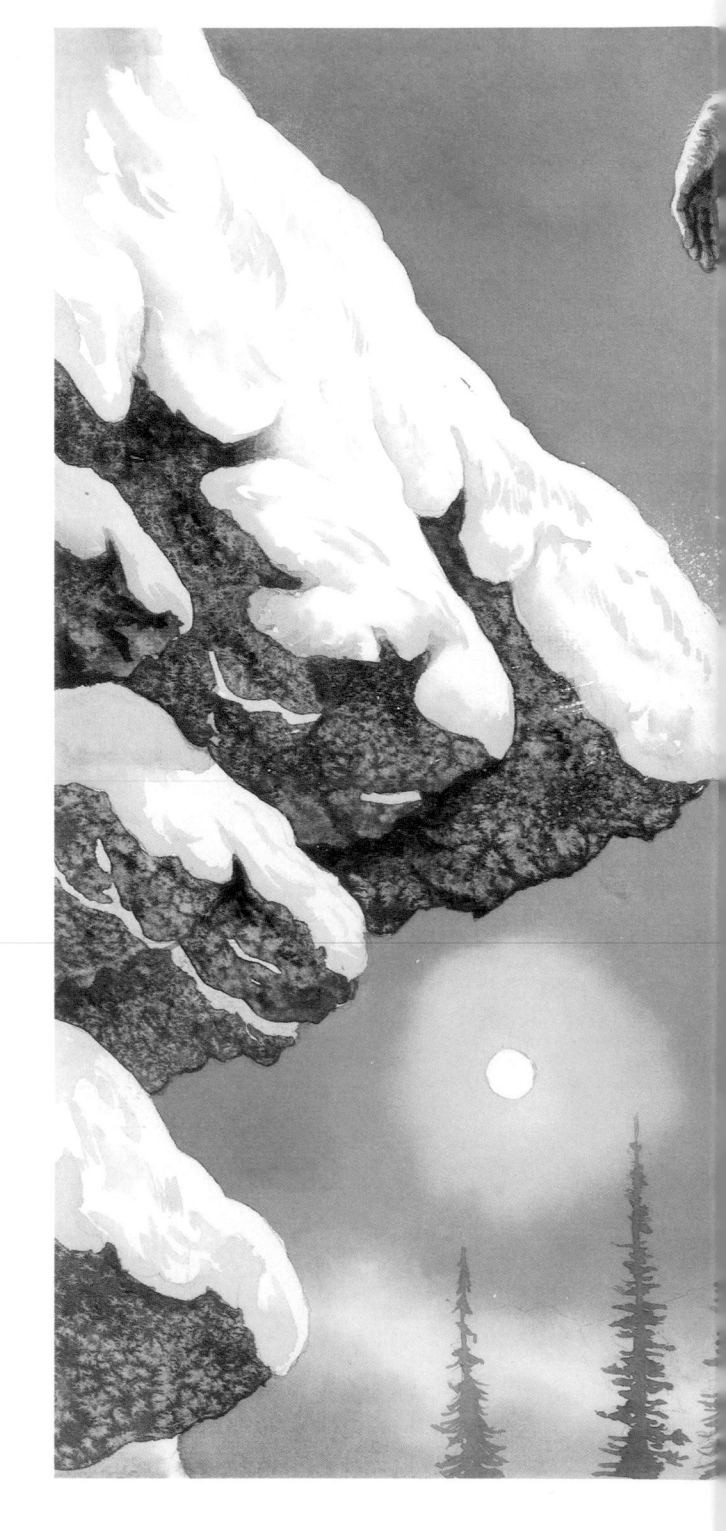

At the edge of the forest we came to a slope.
It was too steep to walk down.

Big Foot lay down and I rode him
like a hairy sledge.

At the bottom was a frozen lake. It was too slippery
to walk across, so we used icicles as skates.

Big Foot was very graceful for one so hairy.

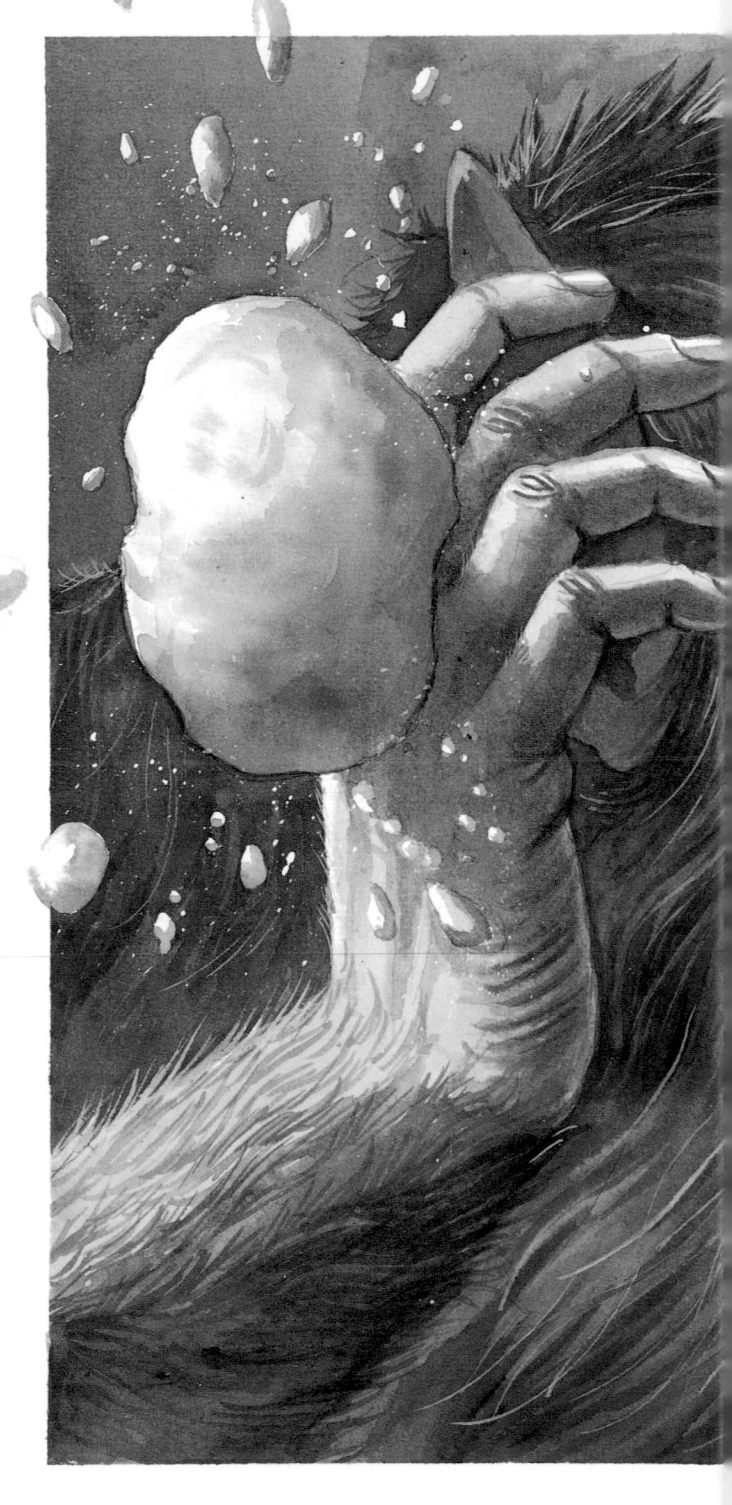

When we reached the other side of the lake,
I challenged Big Foot to a snowball fight.

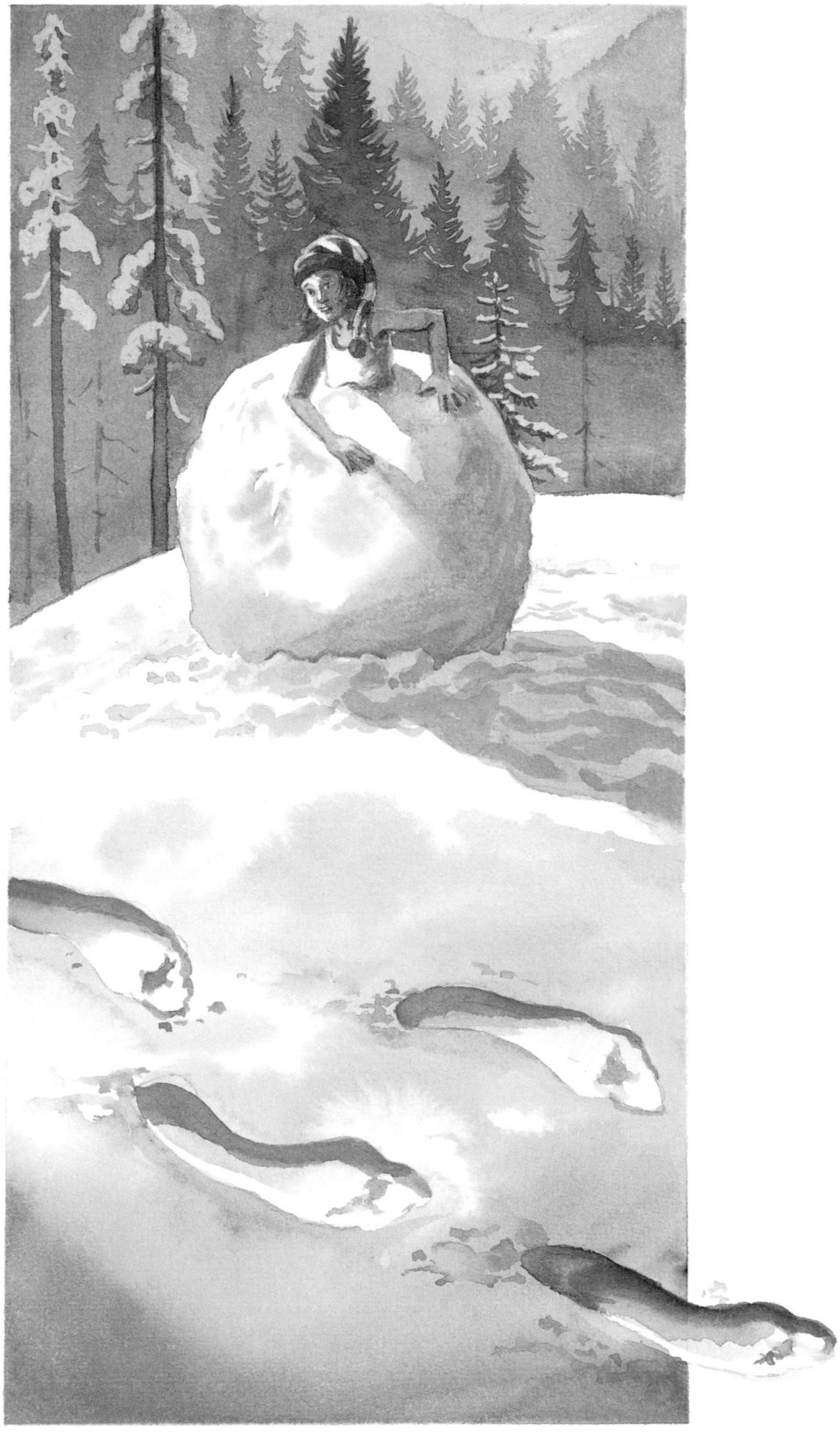

I think he won!

"We should build a snowman," I said.

Big Foot scraped up a mountain of snow and began to sculpt. But he didn't make a snowman – he made a snow Big Foot.

When it was finished, Big Foot looked at it sadly, as though he wished it were real. He wanted another Big Foot – someone to be his friend.

I brushed an icicle tear from his cheek and kissed his hairy face. "I know I'm not a Big Foot," I said, "but I will be your friend."

I suddenly felt very tired. Big Foot rested me on his back.
As we lolloped through the trees I drifted into warm sleep.

In the morning, Big Foot had gone.

That evening I played my flute to the trees,
but there was no reply.

Every evening I did the same, but Big Foot
never answered. Had he been just a winter dream?

Then one fat moon night as I played a tune
to the trees, I heard his song at last. He no longer
sounded sad, and as I played, his song was joined
by another.

Big Foot had found a friend.